Punky Spends
the Day

Punky Spends the Day

by SALLY G. WARD

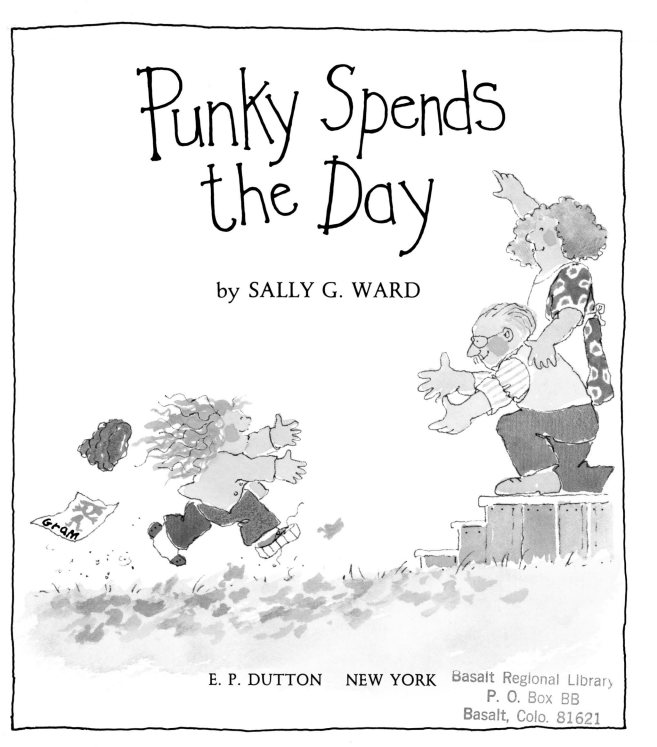

Gram

E. P. DUTTON   NEW YORK

for my mother

Published in the United States by E. P. Dutton,
a division of Penguin Books USA Inc.

Published simultaneously in Canada by
Fitzhenry & Whiteside Limited, Toronto

Designer: Martha Rago

Printed in Hong Kong by South China Printing Co.
First Edition   10 9 8 7 6 5 4 3 2 1

Library of Congress Cataloging-in-Publication Data
Ward, Sally G.
   Punky spends the day/by Sally G. Ward.—1st ed.
      p.   cm.
   Summary: Spending the day with her grandparents,
Punky makes a hideout, rakes leaves, and gets ready for a
bedtime story.
   ISBN 0-525-44526-9
   [1. Grandparents—Fiction.]   I. Title.   89-30550
PZ7.W2158Pu   1989   CIP
[E]—dc19   AC

The Hideout

Punky loved to visit her grandparents.

Their house was full of
wonderful places to hide.

Today she tried all
her usual hiding places

until she finally found
the perfect spot.

Grammy knew just
what she needed
to make the hideout.

When it was all set up,
Punky crawled inside.

She waited

and waited

and waited...
until she couldn't stand it anymore.

"Grammy, I'm lonesome!"

"Hey, where is everybody?
I need a helper."

Surprise!

Raking Leaves

Punky put on her coat and ran outside.
"Grampy, wait for me!"

They raked and raked.

Punky worked hard
at being helpful.

Sometimes
the leaves went
into the basket...

and sometimes
they didn't.

Sometimes
the leaves went
onto the tarp...

and sometimes
they didn't.

They raked for a long time.
"Grampy, I want to stop now."

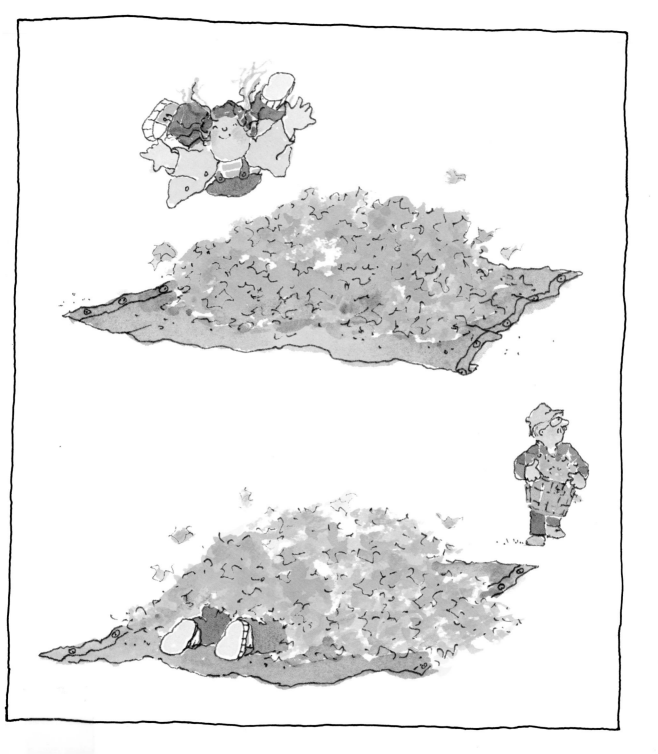

"Goodness, these leaves are heavy!"

surprise!

"Punky, are you almost ready for your bedtime story?"

"Two more minutes, Grampy. I have some things to do first."

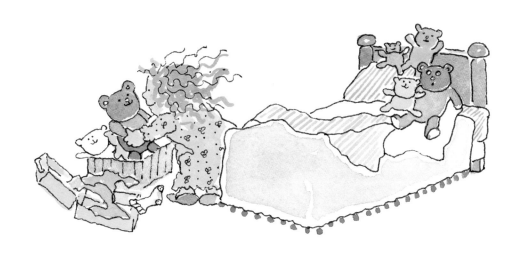

"Punky, I'll be in trouble with your mommy and daddy if you're not asleep early tonight."

"I forgot to brush my teeth, Grampy."

"You'd better hurry, Punky....
We're getting sleepy down here."

"Just one more minute,
Grampy. I have to
pick out a book."

"I'm here!...Uh oh...."

Shhh...surprise.